THIS BOOK BELONGS TO:

A Day WITH MY Dad

At The Beach

By Lance Waite

ILLUSTRATION Manuela Pentangelo

Publishers Cataloging-in-Publication Data

Waite, Lance.
    A day with my dad at the beach / by Lance Waite ; illustration [by] Manuela
Pentangelo.
        p. cm.
    Summary: A father and his daughter spend a day together at the beach,
playing in water and riding rollercosters.
    ISBN-13: 978-1-60131-016-3
    [1. Fathers and daughters—Juvenile fiction. 2. Parent and child—
Juvenile fiction. 3. Beach—Juvenile fiction. 4. Stories in rhyme.]
    I. Pentangelo, Manuela, ill. II. Title.
                                                2007932278

Copyright © 2008 by Lance Waite
Printed and bound in China
First printing 2008

Parents Publishing Group, LLC
740 Gardenview Court Suite 206
Encinitas, CA 92024
United States

This book was published with the assistance of the helpful folks at DragonPencil.

www.DragonPencil.com

A Day with My Dad
At The Beach

This story is dedicated to my younger daughter, Brooke, who loves the beach. When we get there she runs as far and as fast as she can. I really have to race to catch up and stay close so she doesn't get lost.

This book is also dedicated to my oldest daughter, Rachel.

I love you two very much,
Dad

Our cottage is small and close to the beach,
with little white windows and a fence near the street.
I go to school while my dad is at work.
He draws big buildings, while I get paint on my skirt.

After school would be special today, I could feel it inside.
He met my bus at the stop and I smiled with pride.
A day with my dad was the best kind of day,
full of thrills and adventure as he whisked me away.

Once at the beach, I jumped off our bike,
and ran to the water while Dad made the hike.
There is nothing like the warm golden sand
and the sound of the waves as they break on the strand.

I ran down the beach and chased all the birds,
whose flapping and squawking was all that we heard.
When Dad finally caught up, all the birds they were gone
But for a brave few that lingered on.

We played tag with the water, as it rolled up the shore,
exposing new shells, for us to explore.
The point of our game was to stay dry,
but Beegee, my dog, would not even try.

Beegee splashed and thrashed and jumped all about.
When I tossed the ball in the air, with a "go get it" shout,
he'd race through the waves and wrestle it out
then wildly shake his wet little snout.

In the bubbly white water, I paddled around,
though only where, my feet touched the ground.
My dad went with me to be sure I was safe.
He proudly watched over me with a huge grin on his face.

It was time for a castle of grand scale for sure.
It would start as a mound or a big grainy blur.
Begin at the bottom and build to the top,
like the great architect dad, my pop.

Oh, he would design and draw things to scale,
but my plan needed, just a shovel and pail.
I had shells for the windows, and sticks for the doors,
and seaweed and grass, for all of the floors.

We stared at the ocean and listened to birds,
and thought of a future, too good for words.

Dad said, "I love to watch you build castles and swim.
You make me so happy I constantly grin.
You're doing the things I taught you before.
And it's all by yourself, that's what I adore."

"And someday when you're all grown up," he would say,
"I hope that you never forget these days,
they are part of me, in the best kind of way."

Pouring and sifting warm sand on the beach,
Dad covered my body, my neck to my feet.
I looked like a sandy bump near the sea,
And the hot summer sun warmed me beneath.

I finally crawled out of that warm sandy cave,
to completely wash off and ride some more waves.

The sun was so bright and the day so hot,
that the water dried off, as we strolled and we talked.
We walked by the ocean, next to the shore
with shells in our hands. We loved to explore!

While it was rare, it happened sometimes,
that I'd find a small shell with someone inside.
You see, the crabs live in the shells all alone,
and when they get bigger, they find a new home.

Of course, when I found one, that was alive,
I'd lay it back in its place, so it could survive.

Under the pier, we chased each other around
Huge posts that towered over and into the ground.
Dark and scary, shadows abound,
it was easy to hide and not make a sound.

At dinner time, we wandered up top,
to the little stores and the hamburger shop.
They had lots of fun games, and rides on the pier,
a fantastic finish, to the best day of the year.

We stopped for a bite, then went for a ride,
on this giant spinning wheel, that went high in the sky.
We rode it back down, all the way to the ground
then jumped in tea cups that spun all around.

Finally, we had enough.
We walked on back, and gathered our stuff.
As the sun set, in the blue summer sky,
we waved to the gulls, and they squawked goodbye.

We talked a bit more, as we peddled our bike,
about the importance of family and friends in our life.
Dad said, "There is nothing like family, friends and the sun,
to warm the heart and the soul, and to make a day fun."

After a nice warm bath, I snuggled in bed,
and imagined the story, my daddy read,
but the words just faded, away in my head.

I stretched out my legs, as his story unfurled
Then I fell asleep, not a care in the world.

THE END

This is me !

my dog begee!!!

I went to the Beach
with my super Dad

we ride to
the beach
with our
Tandem

Do kite flying, picnics, and spying on a buffalo herd sound like fun? Then you and your child will love the grand hiking adventure in Lance Waite's first book, "A Day with My Dad". Join the author and his oldest daughter as they explore mountaintop wildlife and beautiful scenery on their grandest day out. Through vivid illustrations and an exciting story, children learn that fun and laughter are only a hike away!

Check it out at: www.aDayWithMyDad.com

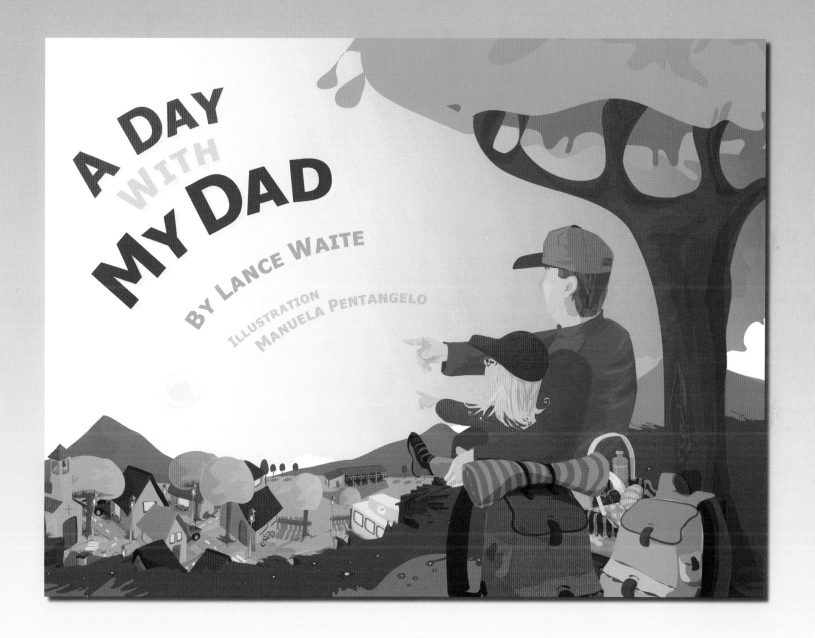

A Day
with
My Dad

by Lance Waite

Illustration
Manuela Pentangelo